D1099972

This Topsy and Tim book belongs to

_____

This title was previously published as part of the Topsy and Tim Learnabout series
Published by Ladybird Books Ltd
80 Strand London WC2R ORL
A Penguin Company

001

978 0 72328 057 6

Printed in Italy

Topsy+Tim

Go to
the Park

Jean and **Gareth Adamson**

One sunny day, Topsy and Tim and
Mummy set off for the park with a
picnic for themselves and two big
bags of bread for the ducks.

The ducks were pleased to see
Topsy and Tim.

Feeding the ducks made Topsy and Tim feel hungry.
"Let's go and find a place to have our picnic," said Mummy.

They ate their picnic
sitting on a park
bench. Topsy had
peanut butter
sandwiches, crisps
and some orange
juice. Tim had
marmite sandwiches,
crisps and apple juice.

When they had finished, there was
a lot of rubbish left.
"What do we do with that?"
asked Mummy.
"Put it in the bin!" shouted Topsy
and Tim.
"Let's go to the swings now," said Tim.
"I'll race you there," said Topsy, and
off they ran.

When they reached the playground,
it was already full of children.
All the swings were taken.

"Hello, Topsy and Tim," called someone high in the air. It was their schoolfriend Kerry on one of the swings.
"Hello, Kerry!" called Topsy, running towards her.

Kerry's mum grabbed
Topsy and pulled her back.
"You nearly got bumped
on the head," she said.
"You must never go
close to swings,"
said Mummy.

It wasn't long before
Topsy and Tim and
Kerry were having
lovely swings
together, all in
a row.

"Now let's have a go on the seesaw," said Tim, when they were tired of swinging. Topsy and Kerry sat at one end of the seesaw and Tim sat at the other, but Tim got stuck up in the air.

The seesaw wouldn't work with all three on it together, so they had to take turns. Then they all went down the slide together.

At last they
had had
enough fun in
the playground. They
wandered back to the
grassy part of the park.
"I wish we'd brought a ball
to play with," said Tim.

"Surprise, surprise," said Kerry's
mum and she opened her bag and
tipped out a big, bouncy ball. Soon
Tim and Kerry and Topsy were hot
and happy, playing ball
on the grass.

Suddenly a big dog came running
across the grass. It caught the ball in
its mouth and leaped around with it.
"Drop it!" said Tim in a stern voice.
The dog dropped the ball and stood
wagging its tail.

"Good dog," said Tim and he put out his hand to pat the dog.
"Don't touch the dog, Tim," said Mummy. "You must never pat a strange dog. It might bite you."

"I wish that dog would go away,"
grumbled Topsy.
"It's spoiled our game of football."
Just then the dog heard its owner
calling. It gave a cheerful bark
and ran off.

"It's time to go," said Mummy.
Topsy and Tim waved goodbye to
Kerry and her mum and they all
began to walk back to the park gates.

On the way, they had to pass the
park cafe.
"I'm very hot," said Tim.
"I'm boiling," said Topsy.
"Would an ice cream cool you
down?" asked Mummy.
"Ooh, yes," said Topsy and Tim.

Topsy and Tim and Mummy ate their ice creams as they walked through the park. When they went past the pond, a crowd of ducks waddled after them, hoping for a bit of cornet.

"Sorry, ducks, it's all gone," said Topsy.
"But we'll bring you lots more bread
next time we come," promised Tim.

Ladybird

Ladybird has a book for every age and stage of your child's development.

For handy tips and advice about choosing books and apps that are perfect for your child, visit

www.ladybird.com